Sadie's Sukkah Breakfast

D1278641

For Sadie and Ori, I love you —J.K.
For Annie—J.F.

Kar-Ben Publishing
A division of Lerner Publishing Group, Inc.
241 First Avenue North
Minneapolis, MN 55401 U.S.A.

Website address: www.lernerbooks.com

Library of Congress Cataloging-in-Publication Data

Korngold, Jamie S.
    Sadie's Sukkah breakfast / by Jamie Korngold ; illustrated by Julie Fortenberry.
        p.   cm.
    Summary: Two sisters plan a special breakfast in their family's sukkah during the Jewish harvest holiday of Sukkot.
      ISBN 978-0-7613-5647-9 (lib. bdg. : alk. paper)
      [1. Sukkah—Fiction. 2. Sukkot—Fiction. 3. Jews—Fiction. 4 . Sisters—Fiction.]
    I.   Fortenberry, Julie, 1956— ill. II. Title.
    PZ7.K83749Br 2011
    [E]—dc22   2010026182

Manufactured in the United States of America
2 — BC — 2/1/12

Sadie's Sukkah Breakfast

By Jamie Korngold

illustrated by Julie Fortenberry

KAR-BEN
PUBLISHING

Sadie and Ori woke up early. It was the first day of Sukkot and they were too excited to sleep. They wanted to see if their sukkah decorations had lasted through the night.

Quietly, so they wouldn't wake up their parents, Sadie and Ori ran to the back door and peeked out the window. How beautiful their sukkah looked! It was filled with paper chains, strings of popcorn, and fruit mosaics they had made in Sunday School.

They tiptoed outside to take a closer look.
"Let's eat breakfast in the sukkah!" said Ori.

"What a great idea," said Sadie, following
him back into the house.

Sadie got the cereal.

Ori got the spoons.

Ori got the bowls.

Sadie got the milk.

Sadie got the juice.

Ori got the cups.

Sadie got the challah rolls.

Ori got the napkins.

So, Sadie got the cereal.
Ori got the milk.

Whoops—too heavy!

Ori got the bowls.
Sadie got the milk.

Ori got the spoons.

Sadie got the juice.

Ori got the cups.

Ori got the napkins.

Sadie got the challah rolls.

What an elegant breakfast!

"Daddy says that when we eat in the sukkah we are supposed to invite guests so that we can share our yummy food," Sadie said.

"But nobody's up yet, and it's too early to call Grandma and Grandpa. What should we do?" asked Ori. "I'm hungry."

"I know some friends who won't mind getting up this early!" said Sadie. "Follow me."

Sadie helped Ori and all their friends say the blessing over the challah. They thanked God for their beautiful sukkah, their delicious food, and their wonderful friends.

The Jewish holiday of Sukkot recalls the temporary huts the Jewish people built and lived in as they wandered in the desert after the Exodus from Egypt. This fall holiday also celebrates the harvest. Jewish families around the world build and decorate sukkot outside their homes and synagogues and eat their meals there.

About the Author

Rabbi Jamie S. Korngold serves as the spiritual leader of the Adventure Rabbi Program. She received her ordination from Hebrew Union College-Jewish Institute of Religion. She has served as a congregational rabbi in the U.S. and Canada, a street musician in Japan, a cook on a boat in Alaska helping with the Exxon Valdez oil spill clean-up, and an Outward Bound guide. She is the author of "God in the Wilderness" (Doubleday). She lives in Boulder, Colorado.

About the Illustrator

Julie Fortenberry is an abstract painter and a children's book illustrator. She has a Master's Degree in Fine Arts from Hunter College in New York. Her illustrations have appeared in Highlights High Five, Ladybug and Babybug Magazines, and the children's book "Pippa at the Parade" (Boyds Mills Press.) She lives in Westchester County, New York.